Because everyone loves a good story...

Alanna Books

First published in the UK by Alanna Books in 2010
Alanna Books
46 Chalvey Road East
Slough
Berkshire
SL1 2LR

First published in the US by Boyds Mills Press, Inc.
A Highlights Company
815 Church Street
Honesdale, Pennsylvania 18431

ISBN: 978-0-9551-998-9-9
Printed and bound in China

www.alannabooks.com

To R. H. B.,
my dad

A Splendid Friend, Indeed

Suzanne Bloom

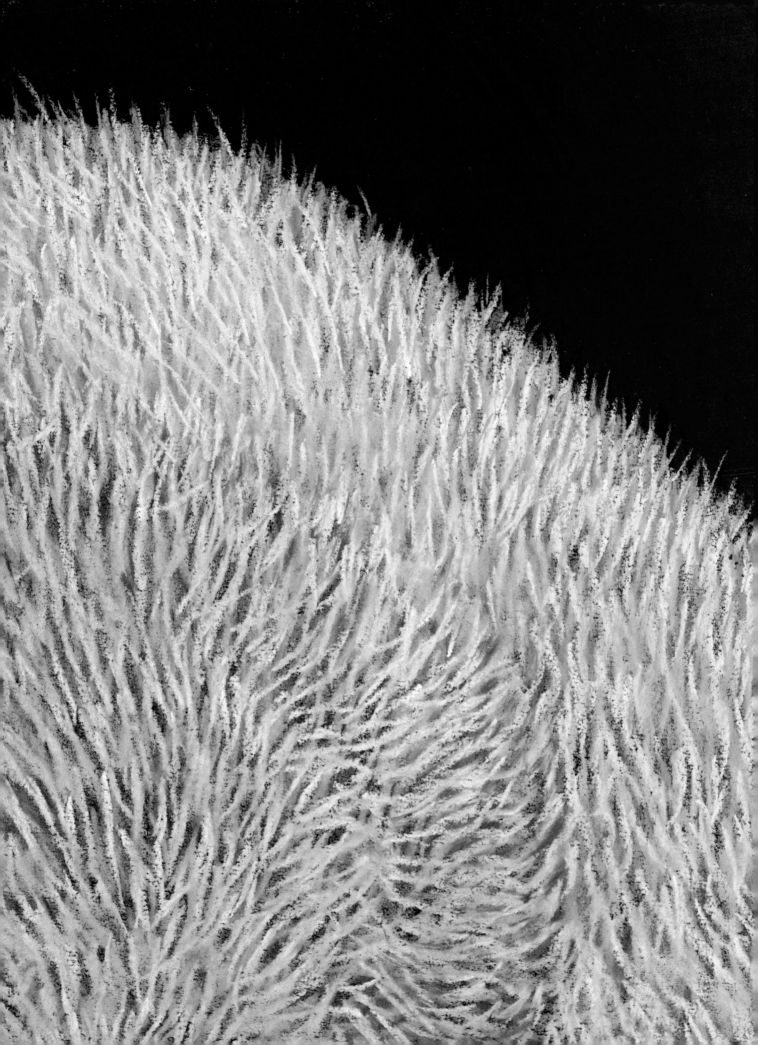

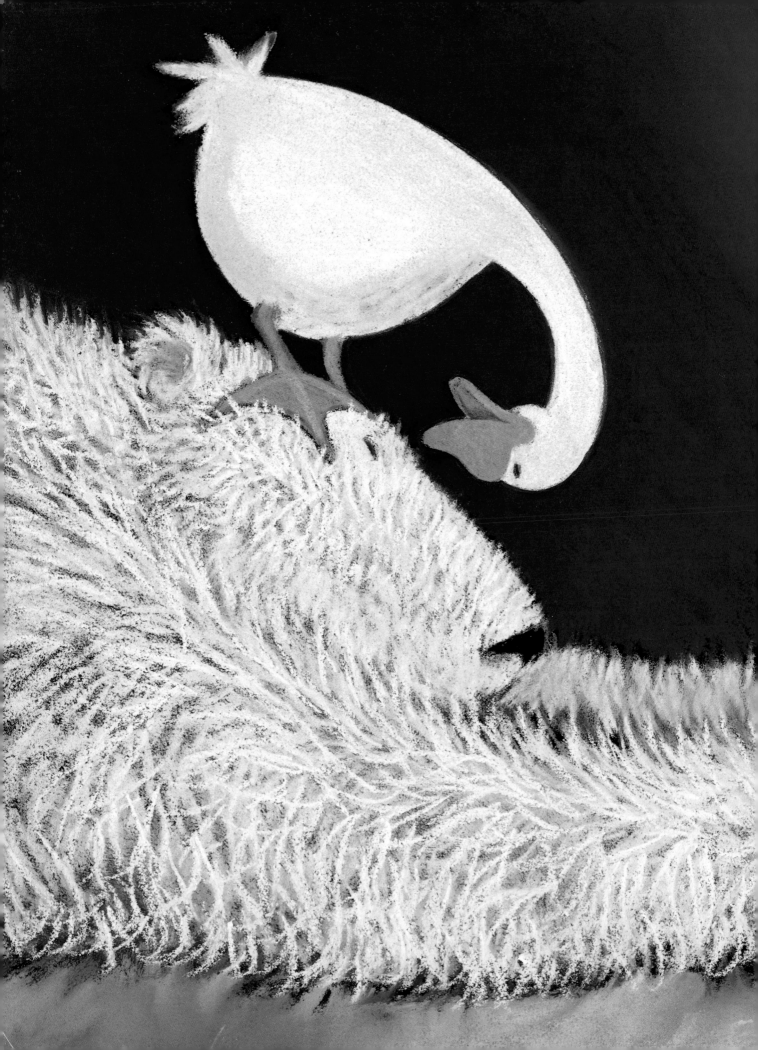

What are you doing?
Are you reading?

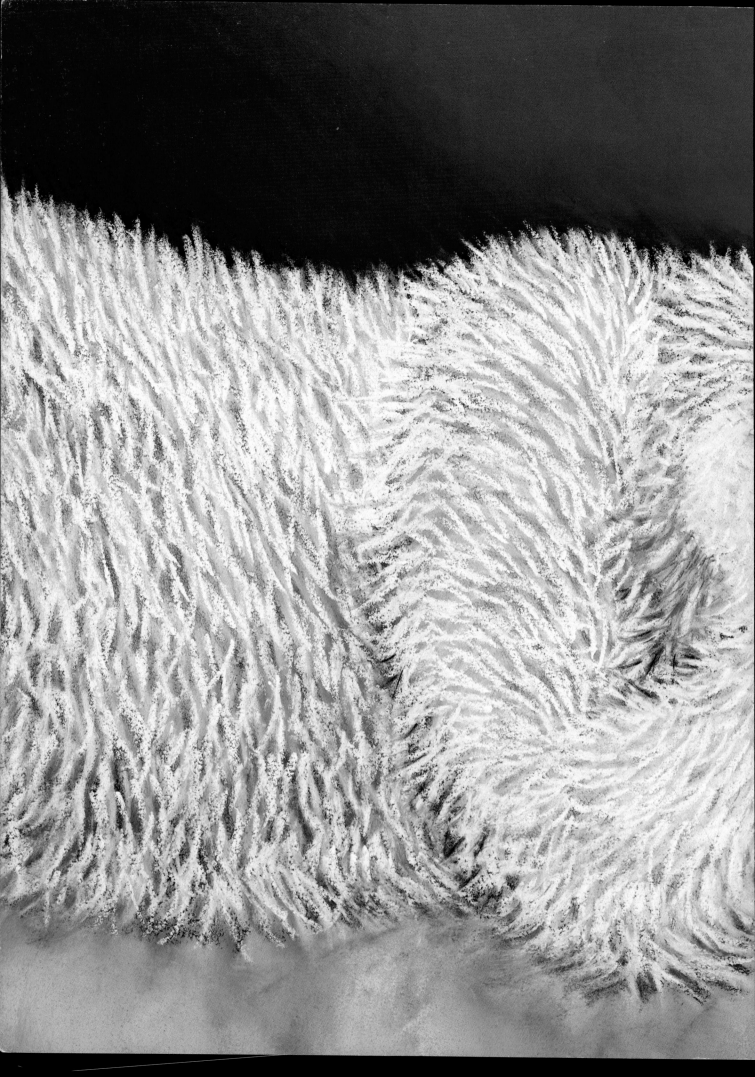

I like to read.

Do you want to
hear me read?

Now what are you doing?
Writing?

I like to write.

Do you want to
see me write?

What are you doing now? Thinking?

Thinking makes me hungry.
Are you hungry?
I think I'll make a snack.

I'm back.
I made a snack.

I wrote a note.
I'll read it to you.

I like you.
Indeed I do.
You are my splendid friend.

Thank you.
I like you, too.
Indeed, I do.

You are my splendid friend.
My splendid friend, indeed.